MARY'S
SONG
A MOTHER'S STORY

MARY'S SONG
A MOTHER'S STORY

M.T. MILLER

Outskirts Press, Inc.
Denver, Colorado

I dedicate this book to my parents
Catherine and Patrick Giebler

Also to
Nanny (Anna M Deitrick) and Francy (Frances A. Thome)

The first people to bring God into my life

Mary's Song
A Mother's Story
All Rights Reserved.
Copyright © 2010 M.T. Miller
v2.0

Outskirts Press, Inc.
http://www.outskirtspress.com

ISBN: 978-1-4327-5537-9

Outskirts Press and the "OP" logo are trademarks belonging to Outskirts Press, Inc.

PRINTED IN THE UNITED STATES OF AMERICA

Prologue

There was a great light that filled the room when Mary was born. Her parents Anne and Joachim thought it was only their utter joy at finally being blessed with a child. Little did they realize this beautiful baby girl was destined to be the Mother of the Promised One of Israel!

Contents

CHAPTER 1

When Mary was 14 her father was concerned for her future happiness. Anne and Joachim were beyond normal age for having children when Mary was born Being so much older then her; they did not want Mary to become destitute and alone. She was a beautiful child with remarkable innocence and grace. Normally it is the man who goes looking for his bride. In Mary's case her father Joachim looked for a husband for her. This was not the normal custom; however Joachim felt it was his duty to secure his daughter's happiness and protection.

Joseph bar Jacob was a carpenter by trade. He was a deeply religious man whose eyes twinkled with fidelity and uprightness. He was well respected and celebrated for his carpentry talents. Joseph was a man that Joachim respected and was very fond of. Joachim sought out Joseph to be his beautiful daughter's husband.

"Shalom Joseph"; shouted Joachim, as he entered the threshold of Joseph's carpentry shop.

"Peace to you also my friend." Said Joseph, and continue; "What brings you to my humble home?"

"Ah Joseph, I have come on a mission of great importance! Have you a moment to chat with me as I go over my proposition with you?"

Joseph pulled up a chair for his friend Joachim and one for himself as well. Intrigued by Joachim's unusual behavior; Joseph musingly asked, "What is this important proposition that is so urgent and brings you here at such an early hour in the morning?"

"Joseph you are truly a good God fearing man; and because of this I have come to ask you to consider a most heartfelt request from me. As you know my daughter Mary is a very beautiful and humble girl. She is grace living and breathing, truly a bountiful gift from God. Anne and I are getting much older and our daughter is very young, but of marriage age. I am concerned that soon she would be alone. The thought of her being alone in these troubled times is heart wrenching to me. So this is why I am here. Please Joseph would you reflect on the possibility of taking Mary to be your wife?"

Joseph was astonished at first. He hadn't had time to think of marriage. When he wasn't working he was praying in the synagogue. For a while he considered the life as a single man; where he would devote all his life to God. No, Joseph never really considered marriage. He watched the sincere anguish in his friend's eyes in anticipation of the only answer Joachim wished to hear. Joseph knew he had to reply with great care.

"Joachim, my treasured friend," said Joseph. "How can I respond to such an immeasurably wonderful tribute from you? I am truly honored by your request. Your trust and faith in me touches my very soul. Mary is, as you say, a beautiful young woman. She would be a jewel for any man to call his wife. Joachim, I have not thought of marriage to anyone at this time. Perhaps you should look elsewhere. I am a humble man of modest means. Mary could do much better for herself. She deserves so much more then I am capable of giving her..." before Joseph could finish what he was saying, Joachim interrupted.

"Joseph, what you say is disrespect to you. You may not have large sums of money, so what! My family and yours have been friends for very many years. I grew up with your father and cherished your grandfather as my own father. You are like a son to me and I believe the answer to my prayer. Yes, I have prayed over this decision for a very long time, at long last, Yahweh has led me to you."

Joseph was still in a daze over all of this. Finally words came back to him. "Joachim, can I pray over this before giving you an answer? As you say, our relationship goes back a long way."

"Absolutely!" said Joachim. "I will leave you now. When you come to a decision we will talk again. Joseph, whatever answer you give me will not change the loyalty between us. Shalom!"

Joseph watched Joachim walk away. He went back to his carpentry and prayed as he worked. Joseph would contemplate all of these things later in his room where he would shut the door and quietly ask God what he should do.

‿‿‿

Joseph's room was more a far corner in the living space of his house. His home was small; the majority of the house was used to make his living. His bedroom was plain, average for the times. There was a bed of hay, crowned by hand woven coverlet. Joseph dropped to his knees.

"Almighty and great are you O Lord our God. Your graciousness and mercy are beyond our comprehension. My God what would you have me do?"

Joseph spent the next hour or so in prayer. When he was finished he walked back to Joachim's house and asked for his daughter in marriage. After he spoke with Joachim he asked to speak to Mary. Mary walked into the room more beautiful then he had ever remembered seeing her. He asked her to sit with him a moment under the fig tree outside her home.

As they were seated Joseph began to speak from the deepest part of his soul.

"Mary" began Joseph; "I have come here tonight to ask your father for his permission to marry you."

Mary was stunned. She too spent many hours in prayer and had not actually thought of marriage. She had known Joseph for many years and loved him dearly. Even though he was much older then her, they spent many hours speaking together in her fathers house. She was truly pleased with his request. Because Mary loved God so much and spent so much time in prayer, she was comforted to know she would spend her life with someone who understood and lived that same love. There was something important that Joseph needed to know.

"Joseph, I am humbled that you have chosen me." Spoke Mary in a very demure voice.

"I must tell you something; this may change your mind about

the agreement that you wish to enter into with my father. First you should know that I have always loved you. You are such a good and upright man. I would be happy to be your wife. It is because of this love and respect that I will now tell you what I have not told any human being. About a year ago at the Festival in Jerusalem, I made a promise to God to remain a virgin. I made this promise so that I could live a life completely given to God. When I made this vow, I realized that I would be sealing my destiny; and no man would want me for his wife, if I would not make myself available to him. I do not think it would be fair to you if I do not fulfill my wifely duty to you. I am sorry Joseph; I cannot back out of a vow that I have made to God."

Joseph was astonished to the depth of his soul with the piousness he was seeing in this beautiful young girl. He hardly knew how to respond to this; so he prayed in his heart to find the words, for Joseph too was a virgin. Joseph reached out and drew Mary close to his heart.

My dear precious woman, I will respect your vow to God; will you be my wife?"

Mary gave a gentle nod of yes and the walked into the house to celebrate with Anne and Joachim.

CHAPTER **2**

It was early morning and Mary was awakened by what sounded like a far-off music and a gentle breeze across her face. She opened her eyes to a figure standing in a radiant light. Mary was startled and thought she was still dreaming and tried to awaken herself up. When she realized the vision was still there, she became sorely afraid and ran from her bed to the far corner of her room.

"Hail Mary full of grace, the Lord is with you!" Spoke the voice from the light.

"How do you know my name?" said Mary in a nearly inaudible voice.

"Mary, I am Gabriel an angel of the Most High God. He has sent me to you with a request."

Mary was visibly trembling by now; her voice quivering she responded: "What is it that God desires of me?"

Gabriel replied; "God desires that you should be the mother of the promised messiah."

Mary fell to her knees. Now she was truly bewildered. For hadn't she made a promise to God to remain a virgin. In a puzzled voice she responded; "How can this be for I do not know man and I have promised the Almighty God to remain a virgin. How can I conceive a child?"

Gabriel replied to Mary's question; "Mary if you should say yes, you will conceive a child by the Holy Spirit of God. He will over shadow you and you shall conceive a Son and you shall call Him Jesus."

Still on her knees and in great fear and ecstasy, Mary responded: "Behold the handmaid of the Lord, be it done to me as God so desires."

The Holy Spirit over shadowed her and she fell into a deep sleep.

ᕤᕤᕤᕦ

When Mary awoke she found herself on the floor, and thinking of her cousin Elizabeth. Why was she thinking of Elizabeth? Then Mary remembered that Gabriel said that, "Elizabeth whom was thought to be sterile is now in her sixth month..."

Mary's cousin Elizabeth was much older then she was. In Mary's heart she knew that her cousin would need help. She talked with her parents and made plans to go to her cousin's aid. First though she knew that she had to tell Joseph of all that had happened to her. How would she share this news with him? More importantly how would Joseph receive this revelation? Mary and Joseph had been engaged about four months. They have learned a lot about one another; hopefully Joseph will trust her enough to know that she will be telling him the truth.

The caravan that Mary would join would be coming through Nazareth in the morning. She had a lot to do to get ready for the journey. Mary stopped by Joseph's shop and asked him to come to her home for supper and some wonderful news to share with him. Joseph was intrigued and promised Mary that he would be there at sunset.

It was evening and they had just finished with dinner. After helping her mother clean up the dining area; Joseph and Mary walked outside to where a tall fig tree stood and it cast a shadow in the bright moonlight.

"Thank you Mary for inviting me over for dinner tonight. You said that you had some extraordinary news to share with me. What is it that you wanted to share?"

"Oh Joseph I hardly know where to begin. Do you remember my cousin Elizabeth and her husband Zechariah?"

Joseph responded, "Yes, a wonderful couple but they could never have any children. I know that they have both been troubled by that and wondering what sin has caused this curse."

"That is no longer so, Elizabeth is in her sixth month!" exclaimed Mary.

"Oh Mary, that is wonderful news. God be praised! Elizabeth is well past childbearing years. How is it that she is with child? Mary how is it that you know this?"

"Joseph, what I am about to tell you will be very difficult for you to understand. I am hoping that you trust me enough to know that I never lie, and that what I am about to tell you is the absolute truth."

Shivers ran down Joseph's spine, a sense of trepidation seemed to cloud over him. He wasn't sure he was ready to hear what he was about to hear. Joseph had no clue as to what Mary was about to tell him. Joseph only knew from the anxiety he was feeling that this was not going to make him feel comfortable.

"Go on Mary, tell me what you must." said Joseph.

"This morning when I awoke I saw a bright light, I was frightened at first, but the voice told me that he was a messenger from God, and that I am to be the mother of the Messiah. I asked him how this could happen since I promised God to remain a virgin. The Angel told me that God's Holy Spirit would overshadow me and that I would conceive and bear a son and He is to be called Jesus. That is when the angel told me about my cousin Elizabeth. He said, 'she who was thought to be sterile is now in her sixth month'

The blood drained from Joseph's face. Had this beautiful young woman gone mad? Joseph didn't know what to believe or what to say. His instincts told him to be calm and to pray over it.

Mary however saw his face. She saw the disbelief and she was disappointed in Joseph's lack of confidence in her. Mary knew she was doing God's Will and trusted Him to help Joseph believe and trust in her.

Joseph decided not to press on with the conception side of the story. "So Mary, your cousin Elizabeth is quite far along, will your mother go to help her?"

"Actually Joseph, I am leaving in the morning for Bethphage,[1] I know this is sudden and I know that you are terribly confused

---

1 Bethphage: a small town next to Jerusalem. Information taken from Bible History.com

right now, but I need to do this. I ask you also to remember the many years that we have known one another; please trust me that I am not crazy or lying to you. I am doing what God wants of me, I can only hope that you believe that. I can only trust too, that you know how very much I love you, and that I would never do anything to jeopardize that."

Joseph left Mary's home shortly after that. He gave his fiancé a hug and a gentle kiss on the cheek. He truly did love her, but his troubled spirit gave him little rest. Joseph went to see Mary off the next day and prayed for her safety; but he still could not accept the story she had told him.

Three days after he had found out about Mary's vision, Joseph decided to speak with Joachim and see if he knew about any of this. After all he has to wonder how Mary knew about Elizabeth.

It was dusk when Joseph went to Anne and Joachim's home. He knocked on the door and Anne answered it.

"Shalom Anne; I am sorry to bother you so late. Is Joachim available for me to speak with him?"

"Yes Joseph, he is. Please come in and I will tell him that you are here"

Joachim entered the room, "Joseph my son, what is it that troubles you at this hour?"

"Joachim, I am sorry to bother you so late. I need to speak with you. Is there a private place for us to talk?"

"Joseph, what's wrong? You appear to be deeply distressed."

"Joachim, may I be honest with you?" Both men were now in Joachim's prayer room.

"Joseph, I would hope that you would always feel free to tell me anything that is on your mind."

Joseph took a deep breath and began to speak, "How much has Mary told you about her vision and how do you feel about it?"

"I see now what is troubling you my son. Actually I believe I have heard the entire account. I must tell you that I was also skeptical. My first reaction was one of total disbelief. Why would the Almighty choose my daughter? How could I be so blessed that a child from my loins would be the mother of the Messiah?

Then I remembered the night she was born. There was a sound like distant music and a gentle glow that filled the room. Anne and I thought it was just our joy at finally having a child. However looking back now, I believe it was a heavenly acknowledgement. It was that memory that helped me to believe that Mary is indeed so blessed by Yahweh."

Joseph was taken by the story that he had just heard, but still his heart was troubled. "I wish that I could believe this, my heart just cannot accept this. I am sorry Joachim; I just don't know what to do."

"The law will require her to be stoned if you abandon her now. You do realize that, don't you Joseph?"

"Joachim in spite of all that has happened the last few days, I do love her. I will divorce her quietly and she will be safe from the demands of the law."

Joseph turned to leave; Joachim gently touched his arm. "Joseph, please pray on this and see what God wants of you. Don't react too quickly. Give yourself some time. God's peace is with you tonight and always."

Joseph turned and smiled; "Peace be with you also."

As Joseph walked down the quiet street, his mind and his heart was on Mary and her vision. He was so confused and distraught. Joseph loved Mary more then he had realized was possible. His heart nearly broke each time he thought about divorcing her. He felt he had no other alternative; being a man of the law and a direct descendent of King David; how could he do anything else?

Joseph reached his door and went to his bed and knelt and prayed for a long time and finally went to sleep. His sleep was restless as he tossed and turned. Suddenly his body and his mind felt a peace he had never experienced before. In the silence of the night he heard a voice calling to him, "Joseph, God wishes you to take Mary as your wife. The child she carries in her womb is of God's Holy Spirit." As quickly as it came, the voice left, and Joseph awoke. The peace he felt during the dream stayed with him and he finally was able to feel at peace about taking Mary for his wife.

CHAPTER 3

It was early morning when the caravan arrived in Bethphage. The journey was long and difficult. Travel was safest with the caravan, since robbers lurked in the mountainous terrain of Galilee and Judea and stalked in the hills of Samaria. There were only a couple of incidences, but Mary was kept safe and arrived in Bethphage, unharmed. She waved a farewell to the caravan as it continued on to Jerusalem.

Bethphage was a beautiful village on the outskirts of Jerusalem, and Bethany. Mary had not been to this little village in some time. As she walked along the streets she embraced the sights and sounds and smells of this village. She remembered as a child traveling to see her cousin Elizabeth with her mother and father, and finishing the journey to Jerusalem with them and the rest of their relatives, for the high feast days. As her thoughts took her back to her childhood, she found herself in front of the entrance to Zechariah and Elizabeth's home. Mary called out to them; "Shalom my cousins, I have come to share your joy!"

Mary heard her cousin running to greet her; and Elizabeth exclaimed: "How is it that the mother of my Lord should come to visit me? I tell you that the baby in my womb leapt for joy at the sound of your voice!"

Mary's soul filled with the Holy Spirit as this prayer of praise spilled from her lips; "My soul proclaims the greatness of the Lord and my spirit rejoices in God my Savior, for He has looked with favor on His lowly servant. From this day forward all generations to come will call me blessed, the Almighty has done great things for me, holy and everlasting is His name! He has mercy on those that fear Him in every generation. He has shown the strength of His arms, He has scattered the proud in their conceit and lifted the lowly. He has filled the hungry with good things and the haughty He has turned away! The Almighty has come to the help of His servant Israel, for He has remembered His promise of mercy, a promise made to Abraham and our forefathers so long ago." [2]

There was a great display of hugging, laughter and tears. The joy of God's love filled the air and touched everyone. Mary noticed however that Zechariah hadn't spoken since her arrival. Mary questioned her cousin on this. "Elizabeth, is everything alright with Zechariah? He hasn't spoken since I arrived here."

Elizabeth became silent and then began to tell Mary about how an Angel had foretold to Zechariah about the birth of their child and how Zechariah doubted the sincerity of the Angel's message. The Angel Gabriel became displeased with Zechariah, and told him that as punishment for his disbelief, Zechariah would not be able to speak until prophesy of the child's birth was fulfilled.

᠉᠉᠉

Mary was great help to Elizabeth and worked tirelessly cooking, cleaning and helping Elizabeth with the preparations for the baby's birth. Finally the day arrived for the baby to be born. Since Elizabeth was well beyond childbearing years, the delivery was very difficult. Mary at one point feared for Elizabeth's wellbeing. Finally the child was born. A robust baby boy, whose cry of life was heard throughout the home, as air filled his tiny lungs. The baby was cleaned and wrapped in a woven cloth and handed to Zechariah. As Zechariah took the baby into his arms, he was still unable to speak; but tears streamed his checks and his eyes rose to heaven, and he held his new son close to his heart. It was apparent to all around him that he was praising God for the enormous blessing in his arms.

Elizabeth followed all the prescribed laws and rituals of time for her purification. When her time of cleansing was completed

---

2 New American Bible; Luke 1: 46 - 55

it was time to make her offering of thanksgiving and to present the baby to Yahweh, dedicating the baby to Him as the first born offering.

When they arrived at the Temple and the rabbi asked for the name of the child, Elizabeth spoke up and said his name is to be John. With that there was a fierce rumbling among the elders. Several went over to where Zechariah stood and laying their hand on his shoulder spoke against Elizabeth and said no, the baby should have his father's name or a name of his kindred. There is no one named John among them! The rumbling continued for several minutes and then a voice from among them sternly spoke and said, "No, enough of this! The child's name is John just as my wife has said."

The voice was that of Zechariah. All these months of silence were now ended and the great blessing of God complete. When Zechariah realized he could speak, a great prayer of praise broke forth from his lips.

"Blessed be the God of Israel; he has come to his people and set them free. He has raised up for us a mighty savior, born of the house of his servant David. Through his holy prophets he promised of old that he would save us from our enemies, from the hands of those who hate us. He promised to show mercy to our fathers and to remember his covenant. This was the oath he swore to our father Abraham; to set us free from the hands of our enemies, free to worship him without fear, holy and righteous in his sight all the days of our life. You my child shall be called the prophet of the Most High; for you will go before the Lord to prepare his way, to give his people knowledge of salvation by the forgiveness of their sins. In the tender compassion of our God, the dawn from on high shall break upon us, to shine on those who dwell in darkness and the shadow of death, and to guide our feet into the way of peace."[3]

Tears of joy streamed down Mary's fair face as she became

---

3 New American Bible; Luke 1: 68 - 79

overwhelmed with joy at these miracles before her. While she was taking in all the joy and love in the temple, she felt a familiar touch to her arm. A bit startled she turned to see the strong tear streaked face of Joseph looking upon her as though he had seen a vision. Mary smiled and embraced his strong arm as she smiled at him with obvious delight that he was able to share this moment.

When the ceremony was over, there was a great gathering of people following the happy family home to celebrate the great gift that God has given them. Joseph and Mary walked arm in arm following the crowd to Zechariah's home. As they walked they spoke.

"Joseph, I am so glad that you are here. What made you decide to come?"

Joseph still holding the peace of God in his heart had this to tell his beloved bride to be.

"Oh my precious Mary, please forgive me for my doubting you. I am a simple man who never anticipated anything more in this world then sustaining my existence with prayer and manual labor. I have always praised God for his bounty to me. Never have I expected the wondrous gifts that he has bestowed on me in these last few months. Now I stand at the threshold of the fulfillment of his promise that he made to our forefathers. I tell you my beloved, which I stand here before you totally in awe, and I must admit somewhat afraid. Truly I do trust in God's infinite mercy and guidance; yet I hope that I will have the courage to fulfill that which Yahweh has given me to do. What goes through your mind as all these amazing things transpire?"

"Joseph, I too have never imagined such blessings. My mind runs through all the prophecies and the scriptures; and I am amazed that I am to be part of the sacred promise of Yahweh. I am scared that I will not be strong enough to face whatever lies ahead. The scriptures are veiled and I really don't know what my role is supposed to be and what truly lies ahead. I know that I have been given a greater honor then I could have ever hoped for; and that God will guide me and give me the courage to face whatever is to happen next."

"Yes Mary, it is true what you say of the Sacred Scriptures. At one time they reveal to us how the Messiah will come in power and majesty and save us from the hands of our oppressor. Then again they speak of terrible suffering and humiliation of the Promised One. All that anyone can do is let the future be in the creative and wonderful Hand of Yahweh."

"Joseph, where do we fit into this plan? How are we going to help bring the promise of God to fulfillment?"

"Mary, we are going to let God show us the way; we cannot do anything but that. This is not ours to decide, it is ours to follow. How God has decided to use a baby to save Israel will be for us to see later. All we can do is follow the plan that God has for us and to raise this child in our faith and customs; to protect him and cherish him. I have faith that God will show us the way; for hasn't He thus far?"

As Joseph spoke these last words to Mary, they entered into Elizabeth and Zechariah's home.

CHAPTER **4**

The time seemed to go quickly as Joseph followed the marriage customs prescribed in the Jewish faith. Since Joseph's father had already passed on, Joseph built the wedding chamber on to Joachim's home.[4] In this way Joseph's father - in – law also acted as his father. Joachim, knowing all that was going on with Mary; gave Joseph permission to steal his bride as soon as the wedding chamber was completed.

Joseph labored with prayerful love and the honest sweat of his brow. He built this room to the specifications of Joachim, and worked on this in addition to his regular work assignments. Finally the day came that the room was complete; Joseph went to get Joachim's approval that the room was okay and permission to get his bride.

Even though the wedding chamber was built at Joachim's home, Joseph still blew the shofor[5] to alert Mary, that he was coming to retrieve her for the wedding. When Joseph blew the shofor, Mary and her bridesmaids prepared the mikveh (cleansing bath) for Mary, as was the custom for a woman in order to wed.

After the mikveh, Mary waited in joyful anticipation with her bridesmaids, for the coming of her groom. She loved Joseph so very much, and the child she was carrying in her womb, moved

---

4 It is the ancient Jewish custom for the Wedding Chamber to be built onto the groom's father's house and to his father's specifications. When the wedding chamber is completed, the groom's father will tell his son when he can go to take his wife. This is usually done when the sun has set; the bride's maids stay with the bride and wait with her, for they never truly know when the groom will come. Once the groom collects his bride the wedding party begins. Information taken from Harvard House.com

5 A ram's horn is blown to alert the bride that the groom is on the way. Information taken from Harvard House.com

in wonderful expectation as well. Mary and Joseph were about to begin a new life walking in the promise of Yahweh.

The family then began the marriage ceremony. It was a simple ceremony; Mary and Joseph stood before the rabbi and two witnesses; Joseph gave Mary a coin. After receiving the coin Mary said: "Yes Joseph I accept your gift to me." Joseph smiled and said; "Mary bas Joachim is now my wife." With that the rabbi blessed the happy couple and the festivities began. For seven days (this was the common amount of time for a wedding feast.) all of Mary and Joseph's family and friends danced and celebrated. At the end of each day the guest would put up their tents to sleep for the night and Mary and Joseph would retire to the wedding chamber. The feast finished with a banquet for all the relatives so as to sustain them on their journey home; because many had to travel great distances. After the festivities were over, Mary accompanied her newly wedded husband back to Joseph's home to begin their new life together.

Mary was the perfect wife. She was at her husband's side helping him in any way she could. In the morning they prayed and sang their praises to God through scripture verses. At sunset after the evening meal they prayed together thanking God for the day, and asking His blessings for a good nights rest. For Mary and Joseph their every breath was a prayer. The people of Nazareth loved them very much.

As wonderful as their life together was; life in Nazareth was not easy. The Romans were dangerous intruders in the lives of the Nazarenes. There was much unrest and dissatisfaction with the Romans. The Romans were brutal if anyone got out of line. (Out of line usually meant defending their faith and trying to follow the precepts of the law of their forefathers.) More and more these people prayed that God might soon send the Messiah to free them from Roman captivity.

Mary heard their cries, but she kept her secret and did not share it with these people. The safety of her unborn child depended on her being silent. Although she could not share God's special blessing with them, she did think of them when she prayed. Mary wondered what all this meant. It was obvious to Mary that the Messiah was going to save them in a way that these people didn't really comprehend. Even Mary could not quite understand. She didn't really know what her role in all this would be either. All Mary did know is that she loved God and trusted Him. God would take care of all three of them. Mary believed this truth with all her heart. She put her life and that of her family, in God's hands.

ﻝﻝﻝﻝ

Mary was standing with Joseph in the workshop where he was finishing the touches on the crib he was building for the baby. Both of them were very excited for the baby was due any day now. Anne had just left. She and her daughter just finished the coverlet for the crib and Mary took it out to the shop to show Joseph. Each was admiring the others handiwork and thanking God for the love that they shared. Suddenly there was a huge commotion going on down the street from their home. Joseph ran down the street to check out what was going on, he spotted one of the men in the community coming back from the center point of the commotion. "What's going on?" asked Joseph.

"We are being commanded to take a census! The Roman's are demanding that each family return to the place of his ancestors to be counted! It's outrageous! Why should we have to move about our entire family to accommodate Rome?"

Joseph, stunned didn't reply; there were no words that could sum the fear and anguish that suddenly gripped at his heart. He read the decree with his own eyes. Everything that the man told him was true. What would he tell Mary? How would he tell Mary? The baby would come at any time now. She is so big with child, how could she make this trip without harming herself or the baby.

Many were the questions that entered Joseph's mind as he walked back to their home. As Joseph walked in the door he saw Mary kneading a ball of flour for bread for their meal. She spotted Joseph and covered the ball with cloth and greeted his return. "What was all the commotion about out there, Joseph?"

"Mary, there is going to be a census. It is mandated by Rome. We are required to go to Bethlehem within the next day."

"What happens if we do not go?" asked Mary.

Joseph's reply was gentle but firm. "Mary, there isn't a choice. If we do not go the Romans will arrest us and sell us into slavery or worst. It is a long trip and we will need to travel alone for the most part, we cannot wait for a caravan and most of the families here are from Galilee. As each family returns to the towns of their ancestry, the group will dwindle and we will be making the largest stretch of the journey by ourselves. Fortunately your father and mother will be accompanying us, since they too are of the line of David."

Mary and Joseph finished their meal and went over to discuss the travel arrangements with Anne and Joachim. Anne was extremely concerned for Mary's well being as well as for the child soon to be born. "We will need to travel light; the journey will take us at very least three days. Joachim, are any relatives there that might be able to put us up for a few days or more?" asked Joseph.

Joachim pondered a moment and replied, "There is no one that I can think of. Our closest relatives have scattered throughout Israel. Most have stayed in Judea, but alas none that I know of still reside in Bethlehem."

Joseph said to Anne and Joachim, "We will leave at daybreak, pack up everything we will need, also any proof of ancestry. This won't be a pleasure trip, for whatever reason the Romans want to know how many Jews there are and the tribes that we belong to; I suspect that they will be difficult on us to prove who we claim to be." Turning to Mary he spoke with great compassion. "I will gather everything and pack up the donkey as light as possible so that you will be able to ride instead of walk. I praise God that your mother will be with us on this journey to give you the extra consolation that you need right now. I wish with all my heart that I could spare you this burden."

The couple headed for their home after bidding Anne and Joachim a good sleep and a promise to meet them at their home at daybreak.

Joseph was holding Mary close to him as they walked. He felt her trembling. "Are you okay my beloved?"

"I'm okay Joseph, I am just a little frightened of this whole trip business. I know that both God and you will keep the baby and me safe. I am just so tired that I don't want to be a burden to anyone else either. It's just silly thoughts that are rumbling through my mind." Joseph gave Mary a gentle squeeze as they walked into their home for the night.

When morning broke the two couples were loaded up with bare essentials as they began their sixty mile journey to Bethlehem. Mary was saddened to leave the beautiful crib behind, she had hoped with all her heart to have the blessed babe sleep his first night, in the beautiful crib, that Joseph had made with such love and skill. The only solace was that they were able to take the cover that Anne and she had made to keep the baby warm. There was little doubt in Mary's mind that the baby would be born soon. She only prayed that she would make it to Bethlehem before he was born.

The first day would be a rough one. The holy family needed to cross over the mountainous terrain of Mt. Tabor and Mt. Gilboa. Even in the best of conditions this would be a difficult journey; but Mary being so close to having the baby, a great part of this trip would center on what she would be able to withstand.

Several hours into the trip they had already crossed into the mountainous terrain. The air was much colder in the higher elevation; much windier too. The sun though brought warmth as it pierced the chill in the air. Mary was in a great deal of discomfort as she rode on the back of the family donkey. She would spend some of the time walking, but most of the time she sat on the back of the donkey, as the beast of burden slowly trod the road before him.

"Are you okay Mary?" Anne asked her daughter.

"Yes mother, I'm doing okay; I'm just a little stiff. Can you ask Joseph to come here mother?" asked Mary.

"Certainly my dear let me give you the reins for a moment and I will be right back."

Anne walked a few paces away to where Joseph and Joachim were walking.

"Joseph, Mary needs to speak with you."

Without a word Joseph walked back to Mary.

"Mary, what do you need? Do we need to stop and rest a bit?"

Mary nodded her head in confirmation that she definitely needed to stop for a while.

Joseph continued in an ever gentle and compassionate tone; "Mary, there is a small valley ahead, not too far down the road. Can you hold on a little while longer? This would be a good place to camp for the night, it will be warmer and there will be fresh water. Will you be able to with stand your discomfort a little longer?"

Mary was feeling a great deal of uneasiness. There wasn't a place on her body that didn't ache from the trip. She was so sore and stiff, and the baby within her was restless and uncomfortable as well, this only added to her distress. Still she knew that Joseph was right; a warmer air and fresh water would help all of them. Mary knew that even though she was uncomfortable, she wasn't in danger. Too tired to speak she smiled and nodded yes.

The valley was beautiful, located near the plains of Megiddo and at the base of Mt. Gilboa. Early winter hadn't really touched this location yet. The grass in the area was still a deep green and the stream flowed freely.

Mary was extremely tired and didn't want to eat any supper. The men had set up the tent as soon as they stopped. When the tent was set up Mary went to lie down. Anne tended to her daughter and then went to work on fixing something for them to eat. While Anne was tending to Mary; Joseph and Joachim caught some fish in the nearby stream. The supper was humble; they ate bread and fish and some sweetmeats made of figs and dates that the women had brought with them for the journey.

Joseph and Joachim were sitting by the fire enjoying its warmth. Anne joined them as she left the tent where Mary was sleeping.

Joseph greeted her with a compliment; "Anne you provided a wonderful supper, we thank you so much."

Anne smiled and accepted the compliment with grace and applauded the men for the wonderful fish.

"Anne, how is Mary doing? Will she be able to make it to Bethlehem?" asked Joseph.

Anne took Joseph's arm and gave him a gentle squeeze as she spoke to him. "Joseph, my son, Mary is a strong young woman. It is God's will that we make this trip. Mary will be fine and so will the baby."

"How can you be so certain of this Anne?" Joachim asked.

Anne replied with great authority; "Ever since we found out about the baby I had wondered how it was that Mary was to be the messiah's mother, since Mary lived in Nazareth. The scriptures plainly state that the messiah is to be born in the city of David, which is of course Bethlehem. When the proclamation for the census was given I realized it was God's Will that we make this journey. This is how I am so sure that Mary and the baby will be alright."

The men marveled at Anne's wisdom and faith. They stayed by the fire a while longer and then went to bed.

֍֍֍

Daybreak brought a new beginning of refreshed renewal as the two couples prayed their morning prayers together. After thanking God for the morning the two women made some breakfast and readied themselves for the journey ahead. While Anne and Mary were doing this, Joseph and Joachim were packing up the donkey, and going over with each other the best route through the hill country of Samaria. This region of Samaria was well noted for its thieves and bandits. After planning the route the two men prayed together for continued safety, as this would most likely be the most dangerous trek of the trip. Both Joseph and Joachim felt that they should be able to make it either to Sebaste or Shechem before nightfall. Today the concern would be watching out for bandits, tomorrow it will be the mountainous region of Mt. Gerizim.

The journey was long, and winter was approaching, you could feel the chill in the air. There were even a few snowflakes that danced around them as they continued onward. Only a couple of times did the travelers feel threatened by the bandits in the area. At one time a couple of grubby looking men stopped them on the way through Samaria. Joseph and Joachim thought for sure that they would be robbed of what little they had. Whatever their intentions originally were, they looked at the young Mary on the back of the donkey and begged off, and stating they had thought the family was someone else. With that the two men took off into the opposite direction.

The mountainous region of Mt. Gerizim proved a struggle for the family. The terrain was rugged and difficult to navigate; however they enjoyed the history that they were passing through. It was in this area that Abraham was willing to sacrifice his son Isaac. It was also here where God stopped Abraham and provided a lamb for the sacrifice; for Abraham had proved his love to God by being willing to sacrifice his only son, his only child.

Here too they had passed Jacob's well in Sychar; and Jericho and Jerusalem; all rich in ancient history. As they retold the stories of these cities it helps them to pass the time and the drudgery of the long journey.

As they entered into Bethlehem, the sun had long since set; and the evening stars and the moon were already illuminating the sky. The streets of Bethlehem were overflowing, Joseph went from inn to inn, and all were full. Anne told Joseph that they had to find somewhere soon because Mary had already started her labor pains. Finally the last inn offered them a place behind the building.

The innkeeper said to Joseph, "Normally I would not offer anyone this stable, since your wife is in labor this will be better then having the baby in the street."

Joseph had to agree with the innkeeper. He nodded his acceptance of the stable and was going to pay the innkeeper, but the innkeeper replied; "No sir, I won't take money for this room, when I can give you a real room, then you can pay me."

Joseph thanked the innkeeper for his generosity and began to make a bed of hay and put a blanket over it to make a bed for his wife.

CHAPTER **5**

Mary was extremely weak from the long journey and her labor was difficult. Joseph cringed with every scream his wife made, as he waited outside the stable with his father-in-law. Joachim looked compassionately at Joseph, remembering the birth of his daughter.

"It is difficult to hear the screams of childbirth." Joachim said to Joseph as he continued with the memory in his heart. "When Mary was born, the night was cool, not like tonight, but that of autumn. Poor Anne had such a difficult time. I was afraid that we would lose her. Then I heard the baby cry and the midwife allowed me to enter. There she was my beautiful daughter, an aura of light illuminated around her and the sound of distant music seemed to filter through the room. Anne, for all her hard work, never looked more beautiful then that moment."

Joseph gave his father-in-law a gentle hug; however he couldn't carry on a conversation for all the anxiety within him. Finally, after what seemed like an eternity of waiting, the sound of a newborn crying filled the air. Anne came to get Joseph and handed him his newborn son. He held Jesus for the longest time and spoke these words to him.

"My beautiful child, you are my gift from God. I know that you are not my son in flesh, but know you are my son in my heart. Whatever you need or want I will strive to give you. You are the gift of life and I treasure you now and I will treasure you always."

After that, Joseph placed the child in the manger bed, and wept that God's son had no better place to sleep then this. Then Joseph walked over to where Mary lay. She was so exhausted and could hardly keep her eyes open. "Do you hear that Joseph?" It was the sound of singing; suddenly the entire stable was filled with music and light. "Glory to God in the highest, peace to men on earth"; were the words of the song, as Joseph and Mary realized it must be the choir of angels singing from heaven.

Anne and Joachim were outside the tiny stable and looked to the heavens and saw a giant star suspended above them. They knew that they were part of a miracle unfolding before them.

"Anne, what do you think these events mean, and why do you think that Yahweh chose us to be a part of His promise of the messiah?" asked Joachim.

"I'm not sure why we were chosen Joachim, but I am sure that the road ahead of our daughter and her new family is not going to be easy. Tonight it begins my husband; tonight the world will never be the same again; as the promises of Yahweh come to pass." After Anne had said this, Joachim put his arms around her and both of them prayed for their children and their new grandson, and the trials that lay before them.

It wasn't long after that, some shepherds came up to them and asked to see the baby. Joachim went in; "Joseph, I am sorry to bother you, there are some shepherds here, they were watching their herd when an angel appeared to them and told them about the baby. May I invite them in?"

Joseph nodded yes, and got up from where he was and showed the shepherds to where the baby lay. The peace in the stable was not like anything any of them had ever felt before. The shepherds wept tears of joy as they paid homage to the baby in the manger. They were there a short while and then got up to leave. One of the youngest shepherds, a boy really, had brought a lamb with him. The lamb did not want to leave, but sat at the foot of the manger. The young shepherd looked up to an elder shepherd, who was his father and said; "Abba this baby is the lamb of God." The youngster took the lamb, placed him around his neck and followed the other shepherds out of the stable.

Mary and Joseph found a room with the innkeeper; in whose

stable their baby was born. They were preparing for the baby's circumcision and presentation to the Lord. *(Anne and Joachim will stay for the ceremony of circumcision and then head back to Nazareth. Mary and Joseph will stay until after the rite of purification.)* At the circumcision ceremony *(this ceremony takes place seven days after the male child's birth)*, the high priest asked Joseph the name for the baby; Joseph replied that Jesus is to be his name. Poor Mary had tears in her eyes with the piercing scream of her baby boy. Even though she knew that the law must be followed, the pain that her child was feeling wounded her mother's heart. After the simple ceremony Mary and Joseph went home to their room in Bethlehem. There they helped Anne and Joachim pack up for the trip back to Nazareth.

"Mother are you sure you must leave now?" asked Mary. Anne took her daughter's face into both of her hands and replied gently; "My child you and your family need some privacy. You'll be back to Nazareth as soon as your purification is completed *(forty days from a baby's birth)* your days for completion have almost arrived. Your father and I will make your house ready for the three of you. Now Mary, we must leave in order to travel with the caravan back to Nazareth." Mary and Joseph held on to each other and waved a farewell to her parent's, and went back to their room to Jesus whom was sound asleep on the bed.

While the holy family was still in Bethlehem, there came to see the child Jesus some kings from the East. They brought the child gifts of frankincense, gold and myrrh; and paid homage to the baby Jesus. Little Jesus was a little over a month old. Mary and Joseph were touched deeply by their visit, and astonished by the visitors' generosity to their child; and they realized that Jesus was sent for all of humanity. Mary was reminded of the prophecy; "A bright light will shine to all parts of the earth; many nations shall come to you from afar, and the inhabitants of all the limits of the earth, drawn to you by the name of the Lord God, bearing in their hands their gifts for the King of heaven."[6] A few days after the

---

6 New American Bible; Tobit Chapter 13 verse 11

kings went back to their own countries; Mary and Joseph packed up their belongings and made ready to head to Jerusalem for the rite of purification. The trip was about a ten mile journey.

The day for the baby's presentation in the temple was a beautiful one. The air was crisp and the sun shone brightly, it was a cloudless day. Mary and Joseph prepared themselves for the ancient ritual of purification as prescribed by God through the Law of Moses. They brought with them two doves and two young pigeons for the purification offering.[7] Jesus was wrapped warmly as they made their way through the temple to offer Jesus as their first born to God. After the ceremony, the holy family was exiting the temple when an elderly man named Simeon asked Mary and Joseph if he could hold the child. As Simeon's feeble arms held the child close to his heart he proclaimed these words from his lips; "Now, Lord, you have kept your promise and you may let your servant go in peace. With my own eyes I have seen your salvation which your have prepared in the presence of all peoples: A light to reveal your will to the Gentiles and bring glory to your people Israel." Simeon blessed the three of them and returned the baby back to his mother and as he did so he said these words to Mary; "This child is chosen by God for the destruction and salvation of many in Israel. He will be a sign from God, which many people will speak against and so reveal their secret thoughts. Because of this, a sorrow, like a sharp sword will pierce your own heart."[8]

Mary was troubled by these words but held them close to her heart.

Because the time was quickly passing, the holy family decided to spend the night in Jerusalem and head back for Nazareth in the morning.

_____

7 New American Bible; Luke Chapter 2 verses 22-24

8 New American Bible; Luke Chapter 2 verses 29-35

CHAPTER **6**

The family was sound asleep in the room when suddenly and angel of the Lord came to Joseph in a dream and told him; "Quickly Joseph, take your family and flee to Egypt. There are men who seek to kill the child. You must take your family now and go, go quickly!"

Joseph arose with a start. "Mary…Mary wake up," said Joseph as he gently shook her shoulder.

"Umm…Joseph, what's the matter?" asked Mary trying to shake the sleep from her head.

"We must leave now!" said Joseph firmly.

Mary gathered up their belongings and helped Joseph pack up the donkey. The baby remained asleep through all the commotion and they headed out of Jerusalem. They were quite a ways from town when Mary realized she did not recognize her surroundings.

"Joseph, where are we going?" asked Mary.

"An angel of the Lord came to me in a dream and told me that we must quickly go to Egypt, that there are men who seek to take Jesus life."

Fear gripped at Mary's heart as the words of Simeon echoed in her head. Why would anyone wish to harm a baby? For what possible reason could there be? All these thoughts tormented her as they continued on the longest trip of their lives, for Egypt was about 80 miles from Jerusalem.

✦✦✦

The holy family had been in Egypt about a week; Joseph had found a place for them to live and enough work to sustain them.

They did not know how long they would be in Egypt, they trusted in God to guard them in this foreign land.

Mary was getting water from the local well while a caravan from Jerusalem was coming into the town of Zoan where they were living. As she was drawing the water, Mary overheard the travelers talking about the horrid events taking place in Judea. Mary was struck with terror. She ran back to the home that she shared with Joseph and Jesus. Joseph heard her crying uncontrollably and ran to see what was wrong.

"Mary, Mary what is it? Why are you weeping so?"

"Oh Joseph, the babies the poor babies; Herod has killed those poor babies."

"What babies Mary?"

"I was at the well and I heard some people of a caravan speaking about the slaughter of infants in Judea. Herod is killing every child under the age of two because he heard that the messiah was born, and he wanted to make sure he killed the one meant to be king. He said no one would take his throne away from him."

Mary could hardly breathe, she was crying hysterically. Joseph realized that the warning of the angel came to pass in a horrible way. He held Mary close to him and tried to comfort her as much as possible. Words from scripture entered his heart and he felt compelled to share it with his wife.

"Mary, I know how horrible this is; do you remember the scripture of the prophet Jeremiah?" Mary could not speak, but nodded in affirmation against his chest, so Joseph continued; "The scripture went like this, 'a sound is heard in Ramah, the sound of bitter weeping. Rachel is crying for her children and would not be consoled, for they are no more'[9], Mary, this is the prophecy that has come true." With those words Mary continued to weep bitterly for the little ones caught up in Herod's greed.

In the meantime back in Nazareth, Anne and Joachim had

---

9 New American Bible; Matthew Chapter 2 verse 18

heard the same terrible news. They were concerned for the family. Anne and Joachim prayed intensely for their children and grandchild. Later that night both of them had a message from an angel comforting them that the holy family was okay and out of harms way. The angel further told them that they would not return to Nazareth until God's messenger told them that it was safe to return. This set their hearts at peace. They managed to keep Joseph's house in good order until the family could return. Neighbors questioned the family's absence, but Joachim in his wisdom managed to dispel the gossip that occasionally came up.

♪♪♪♫

Weeks and months had gone by; Mary was still troubled by Herod's killing of the infants. The words of Simeon still haunted her. How many other prophecies like Jeremiah's were there that concerned her son? How much heartache was there ahead of them? Mary knew the absolute joy of being Jesus' mother. Even in the mist of such sorrowful news of the killings, her heart still knew an unexplainable peace. Somehow she knew that although the children murdered cause unending grief for their mothers, she knew the babies were with God. While meditating on these things, the words of the prophet Isaiah came to her heart, "Come to me heedfully and you will have life. I renew with you the everlasting covenant, the benefits assured to David...for my thoughts are not your thoughts, nor are your ways my ways says the Lord. As high as the heavens above the earth, so high is my ways above your ways and my thoughts above your thoughts. For just as from the heavens the rain and snow come down, and do not return there until they have watered the earth, making it fertile and fruitful... so shall my words be that goes forth from my mouth; it shall not return to me void, but shall do my will, achieving the end for which I sent it."[10] These words assured Mary that the destiny of her family was in God's hands; to Him she placed her complete trust.

---

10 New American Bible; Isaiah Chapter 55 verses 3, 8-11

It had been three years since Mary and Joseph had seen their little home in Nazareth. Anne and Joachim kept everything cleaned for their return. Their stay in Egypt was a pleasant one, but it was good to be home in Nazareth.

Little Jesus met his grand parents for the first time since his birth. Anne and Joachim were so proud of him. They sat on the floor and played with Jesus with the toys that Joseph had made for him. Anne and Joachim loved Jesus very much, for he was the spring in the winter of their years. Jesus was an endearing child; love flowed from his being. He enjoyed working with his father Joseph, learning the trade of carpentry, and being helpful to his mother Mary. Jesus was growing each day into a wise and loving young man. Mary and Joseph thanked God each day for the privilege of being Jesus parents.

Life in Nazareth was good. As time went on life also changed for the holy family. Anne and Joachim passed away when Jesus was about five years old. First Joachim died and less then a month later Anne died. This was a very traumatic time in the lives of Jesus, Mary and Joseph; for they were a very close family and truly Anne and Joachim played an intricate part in their lives. This was Jesus first experience with death. Each funeral Jesus watched his mother and father weep in sorrow. Shortly after Anne's funeral Jesus asked his mother; "Momma, why do people die?"

Mary knew that her little one was hurting, for Jesus deeply loved his grandparents. She sat her child on her lap and tried to explain one of the greatest mysteries and sorrows in life. Mary explained to him about Adam and Eve and the first sin against God and how after that all people were subjected to live by the sweat of their brow and eventually face dying. She told him that God promised a messiah to bring life and freedom to the Jews and that all would rise from the dead at the end of time, to give glory and praise to God.

Jesus had no idea at that time that he was the promised messiah. However Mary held dear to her heart the words he spoke to her in response to her explanation of death. Jesus looked at her and said; "Momma, I will give glory and praise to God now, for I love Him very much, also because He gave me you." With that Jesus gave his mother a kiss on the cheek and a giant hug.

⁑⁑⁑

It is tradition for the twelve year old son, right after his twelfth birthday, to go to the synagogue and become a man of the commandments. There is no ceremony, the rabbi was aware of Jesus coming of age and called him to read the Torah.[11] It was a time of great honor. Jesus was very taken with the Torah. The words in the Torah burned into his heart. For this reason, Jesus was very excited about going to Jerusalem for the Feast of the Passover.

"Abba, come on, we need to finish packing the donkey!" said Jesus.

Joseph looked at Mary and smiled, and said to her; "Well my dear, our son in now a man, seemed like yesterday he was only a child."

Mary, responded a little sheepishly, "Joseph he will always be a child to me. A mother cannot seem to see adulthood in her children."

Joseph laughed and gave Mary a hug.

The Passover festival was always exciting to Jesus. He loved the anticipation of seeing his friends and relatives. It was about the only time that he was able to see his cousin John bar Zachariah. Mostly though, Jesus loved going to the temple. The building was beautiful and this year he would be able to join the men in the

---

11 Torah: First 5 books of the old testament in the bible.

inner room close to the holy of holies. Yes, Jesus was very excited about the Passover festival this year.

As they headed out for their three day journey, Jesus spent most of his time with his friends. It was a little nerve racking for Mary and Joseph, but they realized that Jesus was growing up and they kept the anxiety to themselves. After all they were traveling among friends. Everyone helped to keep an eye on each other. When they arrived at Bethpage, John and his mother Elizabeth met the caravan. Elizabeth asked Mary and Joseph to take John with them to the festival. Zachariah was terribly sick and she needed to stay home to take care of him. John was so excited about the festival this year that she did not want him to be disappointed. Zachariah was up set that he could not be with his son on this very joyful occasion of his first Passover as a man of the commandments; however Elizabeth said it would mean so much to him if Joseph would do this honor for him. Joseph was sad that Zachariah was sick, but pleased and privileged by the request. Joseph and Mary took John with them, Jesus was happy to be with his cousin.

When they arrived at Jerusalem later that day, the city was swelled to the brim with people. They were old and young and every stage in between. This was the holiest and most solemn of all the Jewish feast days. Passover was the time when Jews all over the world came to Jerusalem to give honor and glory to God. This was the feast that Jesus loved the most too; not just for the trip or his friends. Jesus loved this feast for the awe and joy that filled his soul every time he approached the temple. He could not explain why he felt this way; he only knew that he was overflowing with a desire that filled his being with great expectation and delight, and a true and zealous longing to be with God. Jesus confided many of these feelings with his cousin John, who shared so many of Jesus' feelings about God as well.

It was Sunday and the feast was over and all the pilgrims were packing up to exit the city and return to their homes. Mary saw Jesus and told him that everyone was packing up and that they would be heading home shortly. Jesus said; "Momma can I stay at the temple a while longer?"

Mary replied; "okay son, but don't be too long."

With that Mary gave Jesus a hug and kissed his cheek and went back to the camp to help Joseph pack up.

They had been traveling all day and were getting ready to make camp for the night. Mary went to find Jesus, and could not find him any where. She caught sight of John and asked him; "John isn't Jesus with you?"

John looked a little astonished and replied, "Aunt Mary, I haven't seen Jesus since we left Jerusalem."

Panic filled Mary's heart as she ran back to Joseph crying. "Joseph, Joseph, Jesus is not with us!" she cried.

Joseph ran to his wife, holding both her arms at the elbows, he asked her if she was sure that Jesus wasn't in the caravan. Mary responded to him that she had searched and asked every one, no one had seen Jesus since they left Jerusalem. Joseph took down the tent and re packed the donkey. The two of them headed back to Jerusalem alone.

They searched and prayed for two days with little or no sleep. Finally on the third day they went back to the temple to see if they could find anyone there that may have remembered seeing their son. As they approached the outer court yard, there was a small group of men sitting in a circle, with a very young man among them. As Mary and Joseph walked closer, they realized the young man was their son. Joseph walked up to the group and motioned for Jesus to come to him. Joseph did this so not to embarrass Jesus. Joseph and Jesus walked over to Mary. She gave her son a hug. Mary was both relieved and angry, she asked Jesus; "Son, why have you done this to us? We searched for you for three days!"

Jesus replied to them; "I am sorry that I made you worry. Did you not know that I would be in my Father's house?"

Both Mary and Joseph were lost for words. They got a room in Jerusalem so as to get some much needed sleep. The holy family headed for home the next day.

CHAPTER **8**

Several years have passed. Jesus was now a young man, an equal partner with Joseph in the family business. Sometimes the work was slow in coming; other times it seemed like they had more work then they could keep up with. Jesus had a natural talent for wood working; Joseph was proud of the beautiful work Jesus could do with his hands. Most of their business consisted of repairs. Occasionally they would be asked to build a chair or table. Jesus loved creating a piece of furniture. He would add a few ornate carvings that always pleased the client. Joseph and Jesus worked hard, but they had fun too. Many times they would plot together to play a trick on Mary. For example one time Mary had just laid a damp cloth over some bread dough. She remembered that she left her weaving unsecured, and so went to attend to it. When Mary returned to the table, the cloth was laying next to the dough and not on it. She looked at it a little strange and decided she must have forgotten to cover it. There was a loud noise coming from the carpentry shop, she was concerned and went to check it out, and so covered the dough again. When she came back to the table, the cloth was again laying next to the dough. "Hmmm" she said; "I know I covered this dough!" Then Mary would hear the laughter coming from out side the house, as Jesus and Joseph watched Mary's reaction to their prank. Mary would look at them both frowningly, and then smile and join in the laughter of the moment. Life was good indeed for this holy family and Jesus always praised God for his wonderful life.

The holy family always prayed together in the morning and the evening. Often as he was growing up, he would hear his mother and father praying silently to God during the day while they were working. Jesus too, picked up this practice. In spite of constant hardships, the three of them were extremely happy and peaceful.

Joseph and Jesus were best friends. Not only did they work and pray together, but they confided in each other their deepest thoughts. They fished together and gathered food for the family. This was a father and son whom cherished one another; and shared an unbreakable bond.

It happened one day while they were working in the shop; Jesus and Joseph were working on a door for one of the neighbors whom lived a few yards away. In the middle of their conversation, Joseph grabbed his chest and fell to the floor. Jesus ran to his aid but was helpless to save him. Jesus called for his mother. Joseph held Mary and Jesus hand together in his right hand. He told them both that he loved them. Joseph looked at Jesus and said; "Son, you must care for your mother now." With that Joseph passed away. Both Jesus and Mary knelt by the body of the man that they loved so dearly.

Jesus was about Twenty-five years old when Joseph died. The funeral was the most heart wrenching of his life. Joseph had been his confidant, friend and protector all his life. It was a horrible loss. However, Jesus did what he always did, he turned his troubles over to his heavenly Father, and in doing so he found peace.

For the next five years, Jesus supported his mother and continued in the carpentry business, thus supporting them with the fruits of his labor.

CHAPTER **9**

The years were lean and times were hard for Jesus and his mother. Jesus though was a truly good son. He supported his mother and labored hard to pay their expenses. Jesus managed to put a bit of money aside for care of his mother. Mary did whatever tasks she could to bring in a bit of money to the household; she was an expert at weaving. Her talents were needed occasionally by those not as capable physically to do that task any longer. Mary didn't like accepting money for what she did for those people. However, the people needing her skills would not let her do it for free. They insisted that she take a little money for her labor, as she was a widow. Mary humbly accepted what she considered was their charity.

For weeks now Jesus felt himself being called by God to a task he was not sure of. Before Joseph passed away, in one of their many talks together, Joseph told Jesus about the angel and God's plan for him. Jesus was always a bit perplexed with the mission that the angel had foretold. Jesus used to tell Joseph; "....but father, I do not feel this mission. How will I know what to do or what God expects of me?"

And Joseph would always tell him that when the time was right Yahweh would let him know.

Jesus now knew that the time was here. He worried about caring for his mother. Yet Jesus knew he had to do what he was born to do. He waited for a good opportunity to speak with his mother about his mission.

Mary was in the house kneading some dough for their dinner as Jesus walked into their home. Jesus looked at this still incredibly beautiful woman whom had given birth to him. Mary was so strong yet so vulnerable; goodness radiated from her like moonbeams on a clear night. She was such a wonderful and caring mother. Jesus thanked his heavenly Father everyday for giving him such an amazing mother; for he dearly loved her. One of the hardest parts of beginning his mission was this moment.

Mary looked up at her son. She was still kneading the dough when Mary asked Jesus;

"What's the matter son? You have this troubled look on your handsome face."

Jesus couldn't help but smile, his mother always knew when he was troubled, or concerned, or planning a new project for the shop. She seemed to know him better than he knew himself. Still with that appreciative smile, Jesus responded to his mother's question.

"Mother, it's time."

Mary replied; "time for what?" As she said this, she looked up at her son and suddenly stopped what she was doing. She spoke again and asked; "Your time has come?"

Mary didn't know really what to expect. There were so many scriptures and so many people reading into them what they wanted the messiah to bring to them. She looked into her son's eyes and knew as he did, that his time had definitely come. Now Mary had to do what she had done all her life. She would give her concerns to Yahweh and trust in Him. For the first time since his birth; Mary would be faced with letting go of her only child and be absolutely helpless to keep him out of harms way. Neither Jesus nor his mother truly knew what lay ahead of him as he fulfilled his messianic duties. There were many references in scripture to the messiah. Some of the references depicted the messiah as a grandiose king and soldier; others made reference to him as a suffering lamb for slaughter.

"When will you leave?" asked Mary as she held back tears.

Jesus saw the anguish in her eyes and embraced her to calm her fears. He spoke to her compassionately as he held her close to his heart. "I will be leaving in the morning to find my cousin John. I heard he is baptizing in the Jordan River and that he has a large following. Mother, I am not sure when I will return, but I will return home here to you. I will leave you the money from the business. I have been saving quite a bit; the money isn't a large amount. However you should be able to buy the basics while I'm gone."

Jesus and his mother conversed a while longer; then she went to finish her tasks, and Jesus his tasks. Together they ate their supper and enjoyed each others presence, with conversation and laughter.

It was very early in the morning. Mary was up before Jesus to pack some food for his journey. What she packed was modest, some bread and sweetmeats[12]. Not much was said as Jesus prepared to leave, there was just that air of acceptance. They had always been a people of faith. It was that faith at work now to help protect them from the unknown way ahead. Mary caressed the cheek of her son as he stood in the doorway and said these words to him; "'I will listen for the word of God; surely the lord will proclaim peace to his people and his faithful and to those who trust in him. Near indeed is salvation for the loyal; prosperity will fill our land. Love and truth will meet; justice and peace will kiss. Truth will spring from the earth; and justice will look down from heaven.'[13] Go in peace my son and may God's angels watch over you." With that Mary kissed the forehead of her son and sent him on his way.

Mary watched Jesus until he was out of sight; then she went to her room and began to pray for her son as she had never prayed before.

---

12 This is a combination of figs, dates, and raisins; traveling food, which would withstand the very hot mid-eastern climate, without spoiling.

13 New American Bible; Psalm 85; verses 9-12

CHAPTER 10

The Jordan River ran from the mouth of the Sea of Galilee to the mouth of Lake Asphaltitus in Judea. Jesus traveled close along the Jordan River, for he did not know exactly where to find his cousin John. The journey was long; Jesus found John preaching near the city of Jericho. John's followers were many; all seeking to prepare themselves for the coming of the messiah. As Jesus approached, John stopped preaching and embraced his cousin with a warm and enthusiastic hug; for it has been many years since they last saw one another.

"John, the years have been good to you, you look fit and strong;" said Jesus.

"My brother, how good to see you. How is your mother?" asked John.

"She is in excellent health, and has asked me to send her love to you." replied Jesus, as they continued their conversation. Then Jesus said; "John, I want you to baptize me."

John smiled at his cousin and said; "Isn't it you who should baptize me?"

Jesus looked deep into his cousins eyes and spoke almost inaudibly, "John, it is the Father's will that this be done. I have walked many miles to find you, and prayed with each step along the way; believe me John, this is what the Father wants."

John nodded in agreement and followed Jesus into the Jordan. While he was baptizing Jesus, a beautiful white dove landed on Jesus shoulder and a voice from above the clouds proclaimed in a loud and dynamic voice; "This is my beloved son, in whom I am well pleased."

John found himself on his knees, until the water nearly suffocated him. Rising back on his feet, John saw the radiance of God shining upon Jesus. Not quite understanding what was happening or what all this meant; John was speechless and overwhelmed with an indescribable peace. He looked to the crowd around him, everyone there saw what he saw; he could see by the expression on the many faces around him; all were touched by the heavenly image before them. When the after glow subsided, no one in the crowd could believe that they saw what they saw. Not one person confirmed to the others around them that they saw this vision of God acknowledging Jesus as His son.

After the baptism, Jesus embraced his cousin and without saying anything to one another (because their spirits were overjoyed by the presence of God), Jesus began his journey into the desert.

Meanwhile in Nazareth, Mary was experiencing her own trial in the desert. This was her first real experience being alone. First she was surrounded by her parents, then Joseph and Jesus. Mary realized for the first time she had never been alone before. Mary knew that no human being was ever truly alone, for God is always with us; even though this did provide her with comfort, there was this unmistakable pain in her soul; almost like a fear of what is to come. For Mary did not fear for her safety or her economic welfare; but her heart did ache for the company of Jesus and she missed Joseph and his familiar ways that would bring a smile to her face in moments like these.

So in her loneliness for Jesus, Mary prayed for his safety and wellbeing, she also prayed for strength to know God's will and to follow His will.

CHAPTER 11

The sun glowed in Mary's eyes; she had fallen asleep on her knees; fallen asleep in the arms of God. She should have been tired, but she felt rested, her legs had a slight cramp in them; but Mary walked it off and forgot the discomfort. Hungry, Mary fixed something to eat; some sweet meats and a cup of warm water and some fresh fruit, and a piece of flat bread.

After breakfast, Mary put the final touches on the robe that she had made for Jesus. She had hand woven the material herself, so that the robe was made without any seams; and made a red dye and colored the garment a beautiful dark red/brown hue. She did not know when her son would return, but making this gift for him, made his absence so much more bearable.

Mary also finished up the wedding blanket she had made for her relatives getting married in Cana in a few days. Mary was putting away the blanket when she caught sight of Jesus walking into view. Her heart skipped a beat as she threw open the door and ran to greet him. Jesus opened his arms to receive her maternal hug; she has always been such a comfort to him.

"You look tired my son." Said Mary, and she continued; "Come inside and I will fix something for you to eat, and then you can fall asleep in your bed and rest."

"Mother, I am not alone;" replied Jesus. "I have brought with me a couple of new friends." Jesus motioned for the two followers to come to him. "Mother, this is Andrew and John."

"Shalom;" replied the two in unison.

"Come;" said Mary. "Come and I will give you a nice meal and a place to rest yourselves."

Mary fixed a modest meal for the four of them and after dinner,

45

gave Jesus his fine robe. It was the most beautiful garment he had ever seen. Jesus thanked his mother and kissed her forehead and gave her a gentle hug. As he hugged her, he told her what joy she has been for him.

They all spoke together and Mary mentioned the upcoming wedding in Cana. Jesus told her that they would accompany her on the 5 mile journey to Cana.

ᒧᒧᒧᒪ

Cana is a small village, much like Nazareth. Everyone knows everyone else, much like a very large family. Along the way to Cana they caught up with Peter, Andrew's brother, as well as Philip and Nathaniel.

Jesus said; "Ah, my friends, how good that you have come."

Peter said: "Rabbi, we wish to follow you. Ever since we met you the other day, when Andrew brought me to you, I haven't been able to think of anything else."

Jesus smiled with great warmth and said; "you are all welcome to join us. We are on our way to a wedding of a relative in Cana. Come and celebrate with us."

Jesus introduced the men to his mother and she was pleased to meet them.

The extra company and lively conversations made the trip to Cana seem very short. There was much dancing and merriment at the wedding feast. Jesus and his followers as well as his mother had a lot of fun. There was plenty of food and wine....at least the family thought that they had procured enough wine for the feast. Mary noticed a commotion where the wine was stored and her cousins frantically talking amongst each other in a near panic state. For the family would be greatly humiliated at having run out of wine for the feast.

Mary walked over to her son an explained to him what was going on.

"Well mother, what do you expect me to do about it? It isn't time yet for this." Jesus told his mother.

Mary's eyes pleaded with him in great compassion, and this

greatly touched Jesus heart. In his heart Jesus heard the voice of His Father acknowledging that he should indeed do this. Mary recognized this and turned to the wine steward; "Do whatever he tells you."

Jesus told the steward to fill the jars with water. They did as they were told. Then Jesus took a ladle and poured some in a cup for the chief steward to taste. The water had been changed to wine, the best wine that had been served yet. Many people chided the host for serving the best wine last.

Mary and Jesus walked from the area that was bubbling with appreciation and merriment.

"Thank you son;" said Mary.

"You are welcome;" said Jesus as he continued to speak. "How did you know that it was time?"

Mary replied; "Son I did not know. I was filled with concern for our relatives, and all I could think of was that you could fix their problem."

Jesus smiled at his mother, whom always seems to know him so well. They walked off to where everyone was dancing and shared in the joy of the moment.

After the wedding feast, Mary, Jesus and his new disciples went north to Capernaum, where Jesus stayed a couple of days and preached and drew many more to hear him. After two days they all headed back towards Nazareth, so that Mary could rest from the long trip. Along the way Jesus stopped at all the synagogues, preaching and healing the sick. They stopped by a mountain side and there must have been a thousand or more people. To this crowd he gave the beatitudes.

Jesus voice was like a thunder in the hills, echoing and piercing the heart with joy;

"Blessed are the poor in spirit for theirs is the kingdom of heaven.

Blessed are they who mourn, for they shall be comforted.

Blessed are the meek, for they shall inherit the land.

Blessed are they who hunger and thirst for righteousness, for they shall be satisfied.

Blessed are the merciful, for they shall be shown mercy.

Blessed are the clean of heart, for they shall see God.

Blessed are the peacemakers, for they shall be called children of God.

Blessed are they, who are persecuted for the sake of righteousness, for theirs is the kingdom of heaven.

Blessed are you when they insult you and utter every kind of false evil against you, because of me. Rejoice and be glad for your reward will be great in heaven, for they persecuted the prophets before you as well"[14]

The crowd listened intently while Jesus preached. He told parables that even the children understood. Mary watched the crowd, and she watched and listened to her son, and prayed and rejoiced in God for having bestowed upon her such joy and such a blessing; that she should be a small part of this wonderful prophecy, that is being fulfilled right before her eyes. Her mother's heart was overwhelmed with ecstasy and wonderment. There were simply no words to describe the feeling in her soul.

Then she heard her son go on to say how we need to depend on God and not to worry; "Therefore I tell you, do not worry about your life, what you will eat or drink; or your body what you will wear, for is not life more then food and the body more then clothing? Can any one of you, by worrying, add a single moment to your life span? Why are you anxious about food and clothes?

14 Matthew, chapter 5; verses 1-12

Learn from the way the wild flowers grow. They do not work or spin; yet I tell you not even Solomon in all his spender was clothes like one of them. If God so clothes the grass of the field, which grows today and is thrown into the fire tomorrow, will he not much more provide for you? O you of little faith! Do not worry what you are to eat or drink, or the clothes you are to wear. These things the pagans seek. Your heavenly Father knows that you need all these things. Seek first the kingdom of God, and his righteousness, and all these things will be given you as well. Do not worry about tomorrow. Tomorrow will take care of itself; sufficient for one day its own evil." [15] Jesus continued; "Ask and it will be given to you. Seek and you shall find. Knock and the door will be opened to you. Everyone who asks receives, and the one who seeks finds; and to the one who knocks the door will be opened to them."[16]

---

15 New American Bible; Matthew, chapter 6; verses 25 – 34

16 New American Bible; Matthew, chapter 7; verses 7 - 8

They had arrived at Nazareth late that evening. Jesus and Mary, and the five disciples, they rested and stayed with Mary another day, since the Sabbath was approaching. On the morning of the Sabbath, the six of them headed to the synagogue for worship, the men entered while Mary took her place among the rest of the village women. As was the tradition; various men in the temple were handed scrolls to read the words of the prophets; accordingly Jesus was handed the scroll of the prophet Isaiah. He took the scroll and searched for a particular passage, when he found the passage he began to read: "'the spirit of the Lord is upon me, because he has anointed me to bring glad tidings to the poor. He has sent me to proclaim liberty to the captives and the recovery of sight to the blind, to let the oppressed go free, and to proclaim a year acceptable to the Lord'" Jesus rolled the scroll and kissed it and gave it back to the rabbi; looking into the eyes of all present and said; "Today these words are fulfilled." [17]

At first there was such silence and all the hearers in the temple looked to one another in disbelief of what they had heard, and then the murmur of anger filled the room.

"What blasphemy comes from your lips? Are you not the son of Joseph the carpenter and his wife Mary? How dare you stand and proclaim you are of God!" Shouted an angry voice; and with that an angry crowd headed toward Jesus.

Jesus, deeply hurt and frustrated looked at the crowd and said to them, "A prophet is not recognized in his own town." With that

---

17 New American Bible; Luke, chapter 4 verses 18 & 19

Jesus walked out of the synagogue without anyone laying a hand on him.

Mary in the hearing of these things was astonished and troubled. Why would these people not accept the goodness of God? Again the flashback of the flight into Egypt filled her mind. Mary knew at this moment that her son would bear great pain in fulfilling the promise of his Father.

Mary watched her son walk from sight, her mother's heart felt to her soul his pain and disappointment. Suddenly Mary felt a crowd around her, taunting her and trying to shame her for what Jesus has said to them.

From a distance the youngest of Jesus disciples, John, saw what was happening and returned to the synagogue. Mary felt two strong hands on her shoulders, pushing her away from danger. At first she thought it was Jesus, and then she realized it was John. As they moved closer to where Jesus was walking; Mary turned to John and said; "Thank you John, I really don't know what I would have done, I was momentarily stunned by the commotion of the people. They have never acted that way before."

John looked at Mary and smiled and said; "You were like a flower among thistles, I just wanted to protect you and keep you from being crushed."

Mary liked John; his youth and energy was wonderful to behold. What Mary really liked about John was his simplicity and purity of heart. In a time when so many young men felt they had to be fearless and tough, John seemed to have a different kind of courage. Yes, thought Mary, this young man will be a true disciple to her son's work. He can be trusted with life and virtue. As she finished her thoughts on John, Jesus and all the people in the synagogue, she heard the familiar sound of her son's voice; thanking John for rescuing Mary from the mob. As Jesus did this he embraced his mother and tears filled his eyes as he thought of what that mob could have done to her because of him.

John realized for the first time how good Jesus is. Here is a man unashamed to embrace his mother or show his emotions at the thought of harm coming to her. Yes John approved of Jesus;

this man had an unexplainable holiness about him. What's more important, John believed that the prophecy of Isaiah was indeed fulfilled in this man. Yes, thought John, it is good to follow Jesus.

Jesus took his mother's hands into his hands and said to her; "Mother, it is too dangerous for you to be alone for a while. Let us go with you to pack up a few things and we will take you to see Lazarus and his two sisters, Mary and Martha in Bethany. I know they will let you stay with them for as long as you need to"

Mary didn't argue, she nodded and agreed. What she saw today was something she was not used to. Never before in the quiet town of Nazareth did she see the townspeople strike out at one another and react as they did today toward Jesus and her. They arrived at the humble home that she and Joseph had shared for so many years. Mary packed up a few things; they did not stay the night there for fear of the neighbors. For the first time Mary knew what her ancestors felt like as they fled from Egypt to the promise land.

Unfortunately this was to be the beginning of many unpleasant incidences that she would experience at the hands of her people. Mary would find that this journey with Jesus would show her some of the best and some of the worse in people.

The Journey to Bethany reminded her of the journey she made over 30 years ago to visit her cousin Elizabeth. Mary was facing an uncertain future then too. Over the years Mary has continued to put her complete faith in God. Even now, she had no idea if she would ever see her little home in Nazareth again. All Mary knew is that this life is short, and only God and love for Him and His people mattered. Everything else would wither and fade away.

Along the way to Bethany, Jesus preached the good news to thousands of people everyday. Mary noticed that many of them where actually following them to Bethany. There was so much love in the attendance to hear Jesus. She watched as her son cure the sick, and healed the suffering. When he would rest, there were always a crowd of children near him. A momentary sadness attacked her as she realized her son would never know the joy of marriage and family. As quickly as that thought had pierced her, another made her smile, as she realized that all these people were Jesus' family and how he loved them so very much. Mary had indeed learned much about her son's mission in the last few days. What was once shrouded in mystery has now emerged into the light. Mary was so very proud of Jesus.

As the small band of disciples, with Jesus and Mary, entered the area of Lazarus' home, Lazarus peered out of the doorway, when he recognized Jesus and Mary, he called for his sisters and the three of them went to greet them.

Lazarus embraced Jesus and exclaimed, "My friend it has been a long time since I last saw you and your mother! How have you both been? I hear you are stirring quite a following; I am greatly impressed that you have come here to our humble dwelling."

"You have heard then about my mission?" inquired Jesus as he continued; "How do you feel about it? Do you think I am a blasphemer as well?"

"Oh my dear friend," responded Lazarus, "I have always known that Yahweh had something special for you to do. God's light has always shined within you. Please now, come and rest yourselves."

Jesus told Lazarus of what happened in Nazareth and he was more then willing to take Mary in for as long as she needed a safe refuge. They had all been very close friends for many years. There was a great deal of love between the five of them.

CHAPTER **13**

The months and years went by all too quickly. Mary watched as Jesus' mission of spreading God's love and mercy blossomed and matured into a thriving testimony of faith and mutual love for one another. Mary continued on as a guest in Lazarus' home. She stayed on not out of fear of going back to Nazareth, but wanting to stay close to Jesus and his ministry. Mary loved to hear Jesus speak; his words touched her heart so deeply, that she always thirsts for more. She walked many miles to hear Jesus speak, and befriended many of his followers both Jew and gentile. Mary was filled with the spirit of God and wanted all people to love Him and worship Him.

There were unfortunately many times that Mary could not join Jesus and his disciples, because it was not practical for her to do so. In those instances Mary spent a great deal of time in prayer. Since Jesus started his mission, Mary has prayed unceasingly for her son and his disciples. She has found great peace in her prayers and so grateful to Lazarus and his sisters for their hospitality and graciousness.

Lazarus had taken sick recently and it wasn't looking good for him. Martha had asked one of the servants to try to locate Jesus and sent the servant on his way. Days went by and Lazarus situation continued to deteriorate and still no sign of Jesus. Finally Lazarus died and there was great heartache and mourning from all who loved him and befriended him. Mary was puzzled as to why Jesus hadn't come yet; however she trusted that her son was doing the will of God, the Father as she was now accustomed to thinking of Yahweh.

Four days had passed since Lazarus funeral and Jesus had come to Bethany. Martha was the first to see him and ran out to meet him and fell at his feet. "Oh my lord," she said; "if you had been here my brother would not have died; but I know that even now God will give you whatever you ask him for."

"Your brother will rise again;" said Jesus.

"Oh master, I know he will rise to life again on the last day;" said Martha.

Jesus said to her; "Martha, I am the resurrection and the life. Do you believe this?"

Martha replied to him; "Yes my lord, I have come to believe that you are the Messiah that was promised to our forefathers, the Son of God." [18]

After Martha had said this she turned and called for her sister Mary. Mary ran to greet Jesus and in tears fell at his feet. "Oh my lord, Lazarus is gone."

Jesus had loved them all so dearly, and upon seeing Mary weeping, he himself began to weep. "Mary;" said Jesus. "Where have they buried your brother?"

"Come my lord;" said Mary. "I will show you where he is."

When they got to the place where Lazarus was buried; Jesus asked that the stone be removed. Martha spoke up and said, "Lord it has been four days, there will be an unpleasant stench."

Jesus replied to her and said; "Martha, you say that you believe that I am the Messiah, believe then too that what you will witness today will be for the glory of God."

After Jesus had said this and was walking away, Mary, his mother, came to stand next to Martha and her sister. The three women followed directly behind Jesus.

Jesus walked to the sight of the tomb and instructed the men again to move the stone. He again was overcome with emotion raised his arms heavenward and began to pray; "I thank you Father that you listen to me. I know that you always listen to me, but I say this for the sake of the people here that they may believe that you sent me."[19]

After this prayer, Jesus, with his arms still heavenward, shouted in

---

18 From the Gospel of John chapter 11

19 New American Bible; John chapter 11 verses 41-42

a loud voice; "Lazarus come forth!"

A great silence filled the air, and suddenly there stood Lazarus bound in his burial clothing and the crowd gasp in astonishment. "Untie him;" said Jesus.

After Lazarus was untied he walked over to Jesus and bowed before him, but did not say anything, for Lazarus had crossed over into Limbo and was with all the God fearing people who had left this world before him. Lazarus did not speak because he now knew the mission of Jesus and had pledged his silence for the glory of God.

Jesus helped Lazarus up and embraced his friend; then they both then headed back to Lazarus' home.

Mary stood still in awe as she watched Mary and Martha follow Jesus and Lazarus back to the house. Mary regained her senses and followed them also. God has showed her such wonderful things over the years. "Why Lord;" she prayed silently. "Why have you blessed me so? I am always in awe of your mighty works and mercy that you have shown us your people. Why have you blessed me so? That I should be the mother of your Son is still a beautiful mystery to me and I love you so much. My Lord; in stead of asking why, I will just humbly say thank you for this joy and this blessing."

CHAPTER 14

Jesus knew that his days here on earth were nearly coming to conclusion. He truly wanted to spare his mother this pain, but he knew that she would suffer in her heart what he was going to suffer in his body, and his soul. Although he could not spare her this pain, he definitely wanted her to be aware that it was coming. Jesus could not tell her directly, because this was unfolding for him as well; so he determined that scripture would speak for him. He saw his mother out in the garden tending to the flowers. She always looked so fragile to him, yet he knew she was strong and persevered in faith and virtue.

"Mother;" Jesus called out to her.

Mary turned around and smiled at her son; "Jesus, what is it? What can I do for you my son?"

Jesus replied in a most tender voice. "Mother, it has been a while since we last spoke. You look well and as beautiful as ever."

"Oh stop it, you make me blush." Mary replied with amusement.

Jesus and his mother spoke for a while; and then he asked her if she remembered a few of the scriptures that prophesized his mission. She replied that she did and then Jesus asked; "Do you remember this one from the prophet Isaiah? 'He was spurned and avoided by men, a man of suffering, accustomed to infirmity, one of those from whom men hide their faces, spurned and we held him in no esteem. Yet it was our infirmities that he bore and our sufferings that he endured…he was pierced for our offences, crushed for our sins. Upon him was the chastisement that makes us whole, by his stripes we were healed.'"[20]

---

20 Isaiah 53: 3 - 5

Mary responded; "Yes, I recall that prophecy. Jesus, what are you trying to tell me?"

"Mother, I am trying to prepare you for a time of great trial and pain. There are things coming, and very soon, that will cause you tremendous heartache. I wish that for your sake it were not so, but it will come to pass."

"Son, what do you need me to do for you? How can I help you?" Mary had tears in her eyes as she spoke these words and embraced her son.

Jesus returned the embrace and said; "Pray for me mother, just keep praying."

With those words both mother and son knelt in the garden and prayed.

＊＊＊

Jesus stayed at Lazarus home for a couple of days. Jesus knew that Lazarus would be in danger too because of what Jesus had done for him, by raising him from the dead. The Jewish authority would be beside themselves with anger and frustration. Jesus was both saddened and angered by their actions. His coming into the world should have been their joy. Instead they were jealous and threatened by his very existence. Jesus sighed, and acknowledged to himself that this is how it was suppose to be. Jesus prayed to his Father daily for courage to fulfill His holy will. Yes, Jesus is the son of God; he had come to realize that fact; however his humanity wanted to move away from the suffering and death that lay ahead of him. .

It was early in the morning when Jesus and his disciples awoke to a new day. The feast of the Passover would be starting in about a week. Bethany was only a couple of miles outside of Jerusalem; however when Jesus and his disciples went to leave, Lazarus insisted on Jesus taking the donkey to ride on. Jesus humbly accepted his friend's hospitality and rode the donkey into Jerusalem.

As they came into the gates of Jerusalem, there were people standing on both sides of the road waving palm branches, singing and shouting; "Hosanna, blessed is he who comes in the name of the Lord. Hosanna to the king of Israel!"[21]

21 New American Bible; John chapter 12 verse 13

Jerusalem was packed with people in town for the high holy days of Passover. Jews came from all over the world to celebrate this feast in the holy city. Young and old alike were preparing for this very momentous of feast that celebrated the Jews freedom from the slavery in Egypt.

Jesus told his disciples to go to a specific home and tell the owner of the house that they would need the use of the upper room to celebrate the Passover meal. This was done and the Passover meal prepared according to the Law. Jesus sent for his mother and Lazarus and his sisters to join them in the Passover meal. Jesus wanted the people he loved to be with him for this his last supper.

After supper the group went to the garden with Jesus to pray. Jesus was in extreme agony as he prayed to his Father for help to endure all that lay ahead of him.

Mary from a distance watched the anguish that tormented her son, and she prayed as never before. She also prayed for herself, she prayed for strength. Suddenly there was a great commotion in the courtyard. There were soldiers and temple guards, all led by Judas Iscariot. Mary didn't understand why Judas would do this; so she prayed for him as well, she saw Judas giving her son a kiss on the cheek. With that simple gesture the temple guards led Jesus away. Mary cried out for Jesus, but wasn't heard among the clamor that erupted around her. Jesus turned to look at her and their eyes met; Mary knew this was how it was to be. She fell to her knees and wept.

John, still recovering from the shock of Jesus' arrest, saw Mary on the ground weeping and the words of Isaiah trembled from her lips; "He was spurned and avoided by men, a man of suffering, accustomed to infirmity, one of those from whom men hide their faces, spurned and we held him in no esteem. Yet it was our infirmities that he bore and our sufferings that he endured... he was pierced for our offences, crushed for our sins. Upon him was the chastisement that makes us whole, by his stripes we were healed."

John reached down to help Mary up, and he offered his shoulder for her tears. After a while they followed the crowd from a safe distance.

John and Mary were now joined by Lazarus, his sisters Martha and Mary. They comforted one another and prayed for hours as they waited in the courtyard outside the home of the high priest Caiaphas. Mary was emotionally drained; she was helpless to do anything for her son. Even as she prayed to God with every fiber of her being, her faith was being put to the test in a way that it never had before. Mary walked a short distance away from everyone so that she could pray quietly; "My soul does magnify the Lord and my spirit rejoices in God my savior. For He who is mighty has done great things for me...Father, I do not understand what is happening tonight. I have no idea what the daylight will bring, but I fear it will be more pain. Oh Father, please give me strength so that I can be strong for my son; please Father, help me."

For a brief moment an angel come to her. "Mary, you and your son have heaven with you this day, fear not, for God is with you both. Do not lose hope; for this veil is more visible then it now appears."

With that the angel vanished, even in her anguish there was a sense of peace.

The crowd was stirring. The guards were bringing Jesus out. He was still tied up; they were escorting him out of the court yard. Mary and her friends picked up their things and followed. Where were they taking her son? Mary and Lazarus' sister Mary embraced as they followed the crowd. The crowd stopped at the governor's palace. Pilate came out to speak to the Jewish authority and wanted to know what they wanted. There was a bit of conversation back and forth, finally Pilate had his guards take Jesus to the palace where he would interrogate Jesus privately.

Pilate had heard a great deal about Jesus over the last few months, including the story of Jesus raising Lazarus back to life. Because of Pilate's superstitious nature, he did not relish this task before him. Pilate had no fear of men and was capable of the most vicious of deeds; he was however terrified of angering the gods and anyone who seemed to be possessed by the gods. He wanted to end this confrontation quickly. Jesus, however, was steadfastly silent. Pilate became extremely frustrated. "Don't you know that I have the power to crucify you or to set you free?"

Jesus responded; "You would have no power over me at all if it were not given you from above."

Now Pilate was very afraid, this man does have connections with the gods and he wanted no part of it. He had Jesus taken back to the high priest, who was still out in the courtyard of the palace.

"I find no guilt in him; I will set him free and you can do what you want with him." said Pilate.

Caiaphas became extremely upset and said to him; "How is it that you are a friend of Caesar when you let someone who claims to be a king free of punishment? Isn't it said that anyone who claims to be a king is to be put to death? How can you let this man go free then?"

Pilate found Caiaphas contemptible. Pilate also knew if Caiaphas could do this to one of his own people, he would have no trouble in making his life miserable. If word got back to Caesar of that nature, Pilate himself would be given the death sentence. So Pilate ordered the guards to take Jesus back to the palace.

Pilate truly wanted to free Jesus. He asked Jesus if he was a king. Jesus responded that His kingdom was not of this world. This only added to Pilate's anxiety. He paced for an hour trying to find some way to be free of this very sticky situation. Finally he thought of a ritual that is usually done to allow the people to choose who to set free. So he had Jesus flogged to invoke sympathy from the people and brought out Jesus and a notorious murderer named

Barabbas. Surely they would choose Jesus and this mess would be over.

Pilate presented both men to the people. To Pilate's dismay, the crowd chooses Barabbas. Pilate was stunned. He shouted out to the crowd; "You would take this murderer over your self proclaimed king?"

Pilates words fell on deaf ears; for the crowd shouted all the louder for Barabbas. Pilate then had a servant bring a pitcher of water and a bowl. While the water ran over Pilate's hands, Pilate said to all around him; "I bear no responsibility for this man's death. Take him and crucify him."

CHAPTER **16**

The beam of the cross was laid across Jesus' shoulder. Mary watched in horror from the crowd. Jesus looked so weak, she felt like she would faint from looking at the grotesque wounds that covered her son's body. How could he keep moving? He was covered in his own blood. His hair bloodied from the head wounds that the crown of thorns made when it was shoved into his scalp. Jesus, beaten so badly, that he was nearly unrecognizable. Mary could not hold back the tears, her son who only knew goodness was subjected to this cruelty that even an animal should never endure.

Mary and her companions; John, Lazarus, Martha and Mary, continued to inch along the path that Jesus walked. Three times he fell under the horrible weight of the wood. Each time he fell, Mary wanted to run to help him, but knew she could not. Jesus met her eyes several times along this passage, Mary hoped that the love she has for him could be seen in her eyes, and that her gaze would somehow comfort him. She wanted to hold him close to her heart and take away all his pain; like she did when he was a small boy; but she knew that she could not.

The journey seemed endless as she watched her son suffering with every move that he made. Then finally everyone stopped. The guards threw Jesus to the ground and mercilessly nailed him to the wood beam, and raised the beam, with Jesus attached to the waiting wood post. The torture and pain that Jesus was feeling was horrific. Now every breath he took caused him a searing pain in his lungs. The sight of this was too much for a mother to observe; and Mary fainted to see her son suffer so brutally at the hands of such cruel and terrible men.

John cherished Jesus more then life itself, and believed that Jesus is life itself. So what does this all mean? How can Jesus be here and why? John could not take his eyes off of Jesus; he wanted to help his rabbi, his friend. John felt Mary falling and went to grab her. She had fainted into a dead faint; he gently tried to revive her by lightly slapping her cheeks. Mary responded and began to try to stand up; John helped her.

"John, I want to be closer to my son, please help me to get closer to him."

John helped Mary to her feet. Then he and Mary and the rest of the small group made their way to the base of the cross. Jesus was suffering intense pain in his body and his soul. Some of the people were taunting Jesus and jeering at him. Mocking his words and blaspheming against all the truth that he taught them. Then around noon the sky had become very dark and the air very still. For three more hours Mary watched her son suffer. He called out to John; "John, John" and John responded back to him; "Yes lord, I am here, what can I do for you?"

Jesus spoke again and struggled with each word; "John, please take care of my mother as you would your mother."

John responded through his tears; "Yes, lord, I will"

Several more minutes went by and Jesus cried out with all his strength "Father, Father, why, have you forsaken me?" another few minutes went by and Jesus spoke one last time, with his eyes looking to heaven, Jesus said; "it is finished."

With Jesus last breath, the earth shook violently; the people standing around became very frightened; then began the wind and heavy rain.

Mary was in a state of shock, she moved closer to where the body of her son hung, and grabbed the base of the cross where her tears mixed with his blood that freely covered the base of the cross.

Joseph of Arimathea, a secret follower of Jesus, witnessed all these things and was touched deeply by all that he had seen. He walked over to where Jesus mother stood and spoke to her; "Mary, I am so very sorry, I never dreamed that it would come to this. I have a tomb that I had made for me several years ago, it has never been used and it is near the garden not far from here. I will go and ask Pilate for Jesus' body and we can prepare him for burial before the Sabbath begins."

Pilate was only to happy to grant Joseph's request, he felt that this might put him in good status with the gods, of whom Pilate had little doubt that Jesus was of their realm. So then Joseph of Arimathea sent word to his servants to prepare the tomb and to have water and oils there to prepare the body. Time was running out for at sunset the Sabbath would begin. Joseph headed back to Golgotha where Jesus was killed to help the men to take down the body of Jesus.

John. Joseph and Lazarus carefully removed Jesus body from the cross; then they placed his body in Mary's waiting arms. Mary knew she could not hold him long, for the sun would set soon. However she held him close to her heart for as long as she could as the tears streamed down her cheeks and fell upon his lifeless body. After a few minutes she gave the men permission to take Jesus from her and she and the other women followed the men, carrying Jesus body to the tomb.

The garden was very beautiful, Mary, Martha and Mary carefully bathed Jesus and anointed his body with oils and wrapped him in fresh linen. The men then placed Jesus in the tomb and rolled the stone across the entrance. Pilate had placed guards at the tomb on the recommendation of the Jewish authority; so that no one would steal the body. The sun would soon set. John took Mary and the others to a place that he and the apostles stayed on many occasions while in Jerusalem.

CHAPTER **17**

The mood in the small room that John took them to was somber. No one spoke, and the rain still poured into the streets, so that the streets were empty, causing even more silence. Mary stepped away from the window; her mind still racing from all the events of the day. She lightly touched a blood spot on her sleeve, her son's blood. All through these many years, she knew that her son had a mission, and although she had read some of the prophecies that claimed the messiah had to suffer in order to save God's people; she truly never envisioned this. Mary was numb; she had never been so drained in her life. Her poor heart was broken in a way it had never been broken before; she fell asleep weeping. In her dream she saw Jesus, all in glory and radiant; "Mother, do not grieve so. I am with you, always. Remember the scripture passage from Isaiah that we spoke about? The passage goes on to say; 'After a life of suffering, he will again have joy; he will know that he did not suffer in vain…He willingly gave his life and shared the fate of evil men, he took the place of many sinners and prayed that they might be forgiven'[22] . Mother, please do not grieve so bitterly, there will be joy, remember your faith." After Jesus said this to her, he vanished.

Mary opened her eyes slowly and saw that she was reaching out; she brought her arms close to her chest, and meditated on the words of the prophet Isaiah. The words she heard in the dream.

The Sabbath went by uneventfully; the small group was now

---

22 New American Bible; Isaiah 53: 11&12

joined by Peter and the rest of the apostles. The apostles were speaking about how Judas hung himself; and how everyone was still talking about the earthquake that tore the temple veil to the Holy of Holies. It was now Saturday night. Mary hardly said a word all day, no one did. There was an atmosphere of total emptiness; grief so total that it left you completely blank. Mary found a corner in the room and made a place to sleep there. She wasn't tired she just wanted to be by herself and to pray, God has always been her confidant, her friend, the father that she always ran to when she didn't know what to do or say, or like tonight, think. She had spent her whole life for God, most of her life raising her son and helping him in any way she could. What would she do now? What did all these events mean?

Mary could not sleep, after lying awake for hours, Mary walked outside; the streets were still and quiet for it was very early in the morning, not quite dawn. There was a small garden not far from where they were staying; a small creek ran through it. The water flowing over the rocks made a peaceful sound. Mary sat there for a while, not thinking, just listening to the sound of the babbling brook.

"Mother"

Mary looked around, and thought she must be hearing things, for the voice sounded like Jesus.

"Mother" the sound came again, Mary turned around and it was Jesus.

Mary knew she was awake, she gasp with joy and shock.

"Jesus, is it really you?" she said. He held open his arms to embrace her; she ran to him weeping tears of joy.

The wounds on his hands and feet were very evident; her son was standing in front of her in the flesh. Then she remembered the prophecy that Jesus told the crowd, "tear down this temple and in three days I will rebuild it."[23]

"Mother, I cannot stay long;" said Jesus and continued, "Do not say anything to anyone, there are other children who must first

_____

23 New American Bible; John Chapter 2 verse 20

testify to the truth. I respect and honor you so, that I wanted to visit you first." With that he embraced his mother and vanished.

Mary was filled with a joy that she had never experienced before; she stayed by the stream and listened to the water and watched the colors of the dawn, starting to streak the blue-black sky.

CHAPTER **18**

Jesus remained with his mother and disciples for forty days. He ate with them, and taught them all they needed to know, so that they could preach the good news of Yahweh.

Jesus wanted his disciples to teach not only the Jewish people, but all the people of the earth; for he wanted them to understand that all people are God's children. When Jesus finished he knew now his mission had to be their mission.

On the day that Jesus ascended into Heaven, all the apostles and Mary were staying at the home of Lazarus and his sisters in Bethany. Jesus came to them, he spoke with them a while and said that he had to return to the Father now, so that the Holy Spirit could come with the gifts that is promised by the Father.

Jesus took his mother aside and said private words of parting.

He took both of her hands into his and said; "Mother I will always be with you, you will never be alone. The time here will be shorter then you think. I want to thank you for all the love and faith that you have shown to me in this world, and for all the suffering you yourself endured for love of me."

Mary blushed at the complement; "Son, I am just being a mother."

Jesus replied; "Yes, I know; because you are such a wonderful mother, you will be mother of my church, and all of the Father's children will be your children. This is the gift that I entrust to you." With that, Jesus embraced her and kissed her on the forehead as he always had.

He walked away with his disciples and gave them some further instructions. Suddenly he was lifted into Heaven.

人

Mary spent the next twenty years working side by side with John. She aided the Apostles and the other disciples in anyway that she could. Many times she was faced with the danger of death. Mary knew that as long as she held breath that she needed to build the church and spread the good news of God.

One day, while teaching some of the village children, Mary collapsed. John carried her into the house that they were staying at. Mary's body was weak with age and many years of hardships. She passed away quietly.

She was buried the next day, in a tomb at the village. John had come to love her dearly and her death was a time of great sorrow for him. She was a pillar of strength for him in times of doubt and fear. A couple of days after the funeral John went to the tomb. He wanted to say good bye to the physical remains of his adopted mother. When he got to the tomb, Mary's body was gone. An angel greeted John and said; "Mother is home."

The angel vanished, and John looked up to Heaven and smiled, for he could hear the angels singing Mary's song of praise.

LaVergne, TN USA
06 April 2010
178253LV00003B/34/P